at the gym club

Jean and Gareth Adamson

PUFFIN BOOKS

PUFFIN BOOKS

Published by the Penguin Group
Penguin Books Ltd, 27 Wrights Lane, London W8 5TZ, England
Penguin Books USA Inc., 375 Hudson Street, New York, NY 10014, USA
Penguin Books Australia Ltd, Ringwood, Victoria, Australia
Penguin Books Canada Ltd, 10 Alcorn Avenue, Toronto, Ontario, Canada M4V 3B2
Penguin Books (NZ) Ltd, 182–190 Wairau Road, Auckland 10, New Zealand

Penguin Books Ltd, Registered Offices: Harmondsworth, Middlesex, England

First published by Blackie Children's Books 1995
Reissued in Puffin Books 1997
1 3 5 7 9 10 8 6 4 2

Made and printed in Great Britain by William Clowes Limited, Beccles and London

Topsy and Tim were playing in the garden with their friend Josie Miller. Suddenly, Josie turned a cartwheel.

'I bet I can do that,' said Topsy.
'Me too,' said Tim. 'It's easy.' But it
wasn't.
'I can do somersaults and handstands
too,' said Josie. And she did.
Topsy and Tim wanted to know how.

Josie tried to teach Topsy and Tim.
It was hard work.
'I go to Gym Club,' said Josie at last.'
'Why don't you come?'
Mummy thought it was a good idea.
'Perhaps they have a beginners' class,'
she said.

The next day after school, Topsy and
Tim and Mummy went with Josie to the
Leisure Centre. They sat and watched
Josie and her friends doing gymnastics.
'I'd like to do that,' said Tim, watching
a big boy bouncing high in the air and
turning somersaults on the trampoline.

'Look at Josie!' said Topsy, as Josie swung from bar to bar, like a gymnast on television.

At the end of the class Topsy and Tim
met Liz, the gym instructor. She was
very kind.
'Would Topsy and Tim like to join my
beginners' class after school on
Wednesdays?' she asked Mummy.
'Yes please!' said Topsy and Tim.

After school on Wednesday, Topsy and Tim rushed home to change into their gym kit.
'I can't find my plimsolls!' called Tim.
'Where's my T-shirt?' called Topsy.
At last they were ready.

Several of Topsy and Tim's school
friends belonged to the Gym Club
already.
'Hello, Andy! Hello, Kerry! We're
joining the beginners' class,' said Tim.
They all went into the gym together.

'Who will help get the mats out?' called Liz. All the children helped to put them in place.
Kerry turned cartwheels on the mats. 'I'm going to do that soon,' Topsy said to Liz.

'First we'll start with some warm-up
exercises,' said Liz. 'Stand on your
tiptoes, arms stretched up high.'
Topsy and Tim wobbled a bit at first.
'Now jump in the air, like a rocket,'
said Liz. 'Well done, Topsy and Tim!'

Liz made them touch their toes without bending their knees, hop, skip and jump, and then jog on the spot.
Topsy and Tim soon felt warmed-up.

Liz had two grown-up helpers called
Josh and Tina. She split the children
into three groups. Topsy and Kerry
were in Josh's group at the balancing
beam. Kerry was good at balancing. She
walked along the beam quite quickly.
When she reached the middle, she stood
on one leg.

Topsy went along the beam very slowly
and she wobbled a lot.
'Stretch your arms out sideways,' said
Josh. 'It'll help you to balance.'
Topsy reached the end of the beam
without falling off.
'Well done,' said Josh.

Tim and Andy were in Tina's group at
the box. Andy went first. He ran,
jumped on to the box hands first, and
then on to the bouncy mat. He turned a
somersault and stood up, arms
outstretched.
'Very good, Andy,' said Tina.

When it was Tim's turn, Tina stood by
the box and helped him to jump on.
'It's not as easy as it looks, she said.
Tim landed safely on the bouncy mat.
Instead of doing a somersault, he
bounced as high as he could.
'It's like a trampoline,' he said.

When all the children in Tim's group
had jumped over the box three times,
Liz blew a whistle.
'Each group move on,' she said. Tim's
group went to the balancing bar.
Topsy's group went over to Liz at the
high bars.

'These are called the asymmetric bars,' said Liz to Topsy. When it was Topsy's turn, Liz lifted her up and Topsy held tight to the bottom bar with both hands. Then she swung backwards and forwards, higher and higher. Topsy felt like a real athlete.

Topsy and Tim liked all the apparatus,
but Tim liked the trampoline best of all.
The children went on it one by one.

When everyone had had two turns on
the trampoline, Liz blew her whistle.
'Time for the floor exercises,' she said.
'We'll start with handstands.'
With a little help, Topsy and Tim did
some handstands.

'Now we are going to teach you how to do cartwheels,' said Liz.
'Yeah!' said Topsy.
Josh turned cartwheels to show them how it was done. Then all the children had a go.

Topsy tried hard, but her legs would not go up and over.

'Take a little run at it,' Liz told her. 'Then down with one hand, down with the next, legs up and over – and land on your feet.'

They had only five minutes to practise before it was time to go.

All that week Topsy and Tim practised cartwheels in the garden. Josie came and helped them.

On Saturday they put on a Gym Show for Mummy and Dad.

Tim turned somersaults and did a handstand, but Topsy became the star of the show when she turned a perfect cartwheel.